It's Good to be Grand

by
Marianne Richmond

It's Good to be Grand

Marianne Richmond Studios, Inc.
420 N. 5th Street, Suite 840
Minneapolis, MN 55401
www.mariannerichmond.com

ISBN 0-9770000-2-8

Illustrations by Marianne Richmond

Book design by Meg Anderson

Printed in China

First Printing

It's good to be grand!

Could you ever imagine
before you were "grand"...

all the gifts
and giggles

and joys unplanned?

You get a cool
new name
created for you,

whether Nana

or Grandpa

or dearest Mamoo.

Yours is the house
for happily playing...

For LOTS of eating
and overnight staying.

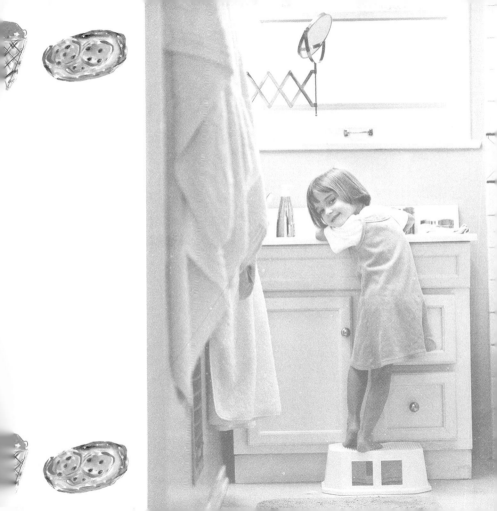

Yours are the arms for hugging us tightly.

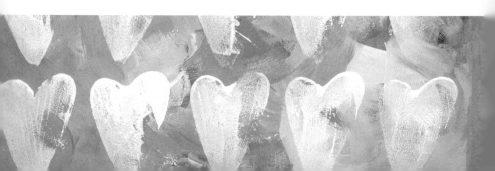

Yours is the voice that tells us politely...

"keep Kool-Aid®
in the kitchen"
and "hands off
the walls."

"Be careful
roughhousing
to avoid
serious falls

It's good to be grand
when you realize you're done
with all the hard parenting
that wasn't as fun...

as this grand adventure,
this wonderful stage
that comes when it does
no matter your age!

Baby Department

It's good to be grand
when you receive a note
and a picture with words
that a wee person wrote:

"I made this for you
'cause I love you a bunch..."

"Can I come over
and eat ice cream for lunch?"

It's good to be grand
when your lap is the best
for a story or snack
or for a mid-day rest.

It's good to be grand
when you can take it all in...

your grandkids' sweetness
and mischievous grins.

You're great.
You're grand.
It's easy to see...

And we

love

love

love you...

Unconditionally!

A gifted author and artist, Marianne Richmond shares
her creations with millions of people worldwide
through her delightful books, cards, and giftware.
In addition to the *Simply Said...* and *Smartly Said...*
gift book series, she has written and illustrated five
additional books: **The Gift of an Angel,
The Gift of a Memory, Hooray for You!,
The Gifts of Being Grand** and **I Love You So...**

To learn more about Marianne's products, please visit
www.mariannerichmond.com.